W9-COZ-668

Lost Aria

Lost Aria

Carmelo Militano

Ekstasis Editions

Copyright © Carmelo Militano 2018
Author photo: Pina Militano
Cover photo: Carmelo Militano

Published in 2018 by:
Ekstasis Editions Canada Ltd.
Box 8474, Main Postal Outlet
Victoria, B.C. V8W 3S1

Ekstasis Editions
Box 571
Banff, Alberta T1L 1E3

All rights reserved. No part of this book may be reproduced in any form without the written permission of the publisher, with the exception of brief passages in reviews. Any request for photocopying or other reproduction of any part of this book should be directed in writing to the publisher or to ACCESS: The Canadian Copyright Licensing Agency, One Yonge Street, Suite 800, Toronto, Ontario, Canada, M5E 1E5.

LIBRARY AND ARCHIVES CANADA CATALOGUING IN PUBLICATION

Militano, Carmelo, author
    Lost Aria / Carmelo Militano.

Short stories.
Issued in print and electronic formats.
ISBN 978-1-77171-312-2 (softcover).--ISBN 978-1-77171-313-9 (ebook)

    I. Title.

PS8626.I435L67 2018   C813'.6   C2018-905406-9
                                              C2018-905407-7

Canada Council   Conseil des Arts
for the Arts   du Canada

Funded by the
Government
of Canada | Canadä

Ekstasis Editions acknowledges financial support for the publication of **Lost Aria** from the government of Canada through the Canada Book Fund and the Canada Council for the Arts, and from the Province of British Columbia through the Book Publishing Tax Credit.

Printed and bound in Canada.

Contents

It's wrong to say I think: one should say I am thought, pardon the pun.

I is someone else.

~Arthur Rimbaud in a letter to George
Izambard, his former teacher.
May 13, 1871

There is no self. It suffices to walk any distance along the inexorable rigidity that the mirrors of the past open to us to feel outsiders, naively flustered by our own bygone days. There is no community of intention to them, nor are they propelled by the same breeze.

~ Jorge Luis Borges

An Oneiric Education

Money was no longer a problem. I had made good money driving a bush cutter mowing down scrub and brush that grew under the telecommunication lines of obscure spur rail lines in northern Saskatchewan. I was also lost and longing for the dull ache of loss to leave me alone.

My Uncle Joe – a section rail foreman – had used his connections to get me a summer job.

—Good hard work and aria frescha will help you get your mind off things.

It's been a bad for you and your sister. Lasci la morte dietro. I will tell them you are coming.

I dutifully arrived Monday morning. The guy at the railway employment office talked to me from behind an old-fashioned tellers grate.

—Can you drive a standard?

—Yes

—Good, he replied. and went away and returned with a long sheet of paper about the size of foolscap.

—Here fill this out.

He handed me the sheet and a bland Bic pen and went away again.

I breezed through the standard form – name, address, and current occupation – and waited and waited.

He finally returned coffee cup in hand and took the form from me and produced another form.

—Sign here. It's for the income tax people.

He then handed me a small square paper with what I assumed was his signature on it. It was a rail pass.

—There is a train to Rivers on Wednesday from there you can get a ride to St. Lazure. Can you leave Wednesday?

Good-bye to city for the summer I thought. My sister Franca was the only one who would miss me.

I ate supper in the one and only hotel in town. After a supper of pork chops with bland apple sauce, bland boiled potatoes and green beans I went for a walk around town and smoked a few cigarettes before making my way back to the hotel. There was nothing much to St. Lazure. At one end of the street was the old two store wooden hotel where I was staying. The hotel needed a paint job. The wood was faded and sun-bleached grey, window frames cracked. Near the hotel was the sealed railway station beside an empty wooden platform for non-existent passengers.

The next day I ate breakfast across the street in a strange baroque building. The place was diner, pool hall, and barber-shop all under one roof and you entered each room from a small door at the end of a narrow hallway and then crossed over from one room to the next. The place felt like a rooming house. The owner spoke English with a heavy French accent and had an immaculate head of wavy-hair. I wondered who cut it for him. At the end of the one street in town stood a lumber yard and hardware shop and a small garage. There was a Second World War tank turret mounted on a homemade three-legged iron stand with the plague that simply said in English and French 'To the dead and returned Veterans.'

I was in a small village that owned the last gasp of its existence to the railway and the lumber yard down the street and in the proverbial middle of nowhere.

Living and working on the edge of nowhere added to the steady bloom of panic and restlessness I was trying to keep at bay. I felt ship-wrecked and abandoned barely clinging to the wreckage of the past.

I read poetry after supper, I was re-reading T.S. Eliot and Dylan Thomas, and later jotted down notes on what I saw in the valley during the day when I was out driving the bush-cutter. Clean unblemished sky. Blue pulled tight and smooth as a drum. Pale ghost summer moon half way between the horizon and the sky in the morning. Sunny afternoons with a lone hawk slowly circling and watching over the vast wide valley. Green oat and barley waves and flutters in the wind, tops of small birch trees at the edge of a forest bow. The CN main line stretches above the valley into the distance accompanied by miles of silence and an ocean of emptiness.

In the silence and spaces before sleep my new erotic experiences returned.

We had been necking in the car when she slipped her hands into my jeans. I was surprised. We were in the car together parked on a street near St. Ignatius Church after the first Sunday of my parent's death. I had gone to pick her up; there was no one else available. It was winter. The car heater blasted out waves of heat and I was having a terrible time knowing what to do with my hands under her turtleneck sweater. I came quickly in her hands; she smiled and laughed gently and then hugged and kissed me. She then wiped her hands on the back of blue faux-fur seat covers. We returned home and said nothing. The sun seemed to shine brighter and softer.

My memory of that Sunday morning was connected to the movie 'Last Tango in Paris.' My sister had taken me to see the film a few weeks before I left for St. Lazure, and many years after its initial release. I guess she was trying to make me mature and wise, to move on somehow.

My sister and I had gone to a few bleak non-narrative existential French films made in the late 50's and early 60's. This did little to relieve the feeling we were both alone in the world but it did reinforce the feeling I was living some kind of version of a French film.

I retuned from my summer job bored and anxious but she made sure I enrolled in university. We both expected university to change my life.

I discovered instead that most students at St. Thomas College smoked and drank coffee and where primarily interested in gossip and endless rounds of Bridge. At night some students found themselves in the library. Many hung around the student lounge, or student council offices day, noon, and night. The ennui was thick.

Weekends and sometimes mid-week students piled into the pub upstairs on the third floor of the Student Union building, constructed like a three level bunker. I usually did not go. My brooding did not make me much of a bon vivant, but one mid-afternoon I did go on a whim and I met Monica, a pretty theater student.

—This is his last year and he wants to go back to Italy. He hates winter here. Imagine that! Go and audition.

—Not so sure about that, I replied.

—Oh, go. Did we break up? Best friend die?

—No. Why do you say that?

—You look gloomy or are you the strong silent type? Really intense. I'm having a party next weekend, 324 Wardlaw Street off Osborne in the Village. Why don't you come?

Monica was both ordinary and exotic looking, thick blonde curly hair knotted and wild, but she dressed plainly: black T-shirt, jeans, and low boots. I liked her open animated manner, her flip spontaneity. She came across as vibrant and exciting. She reminded me of my sister.

—Go to the audition. Thursday over at University College in the basement. Then come to the party and tell me what happened.

Trying acting did not seem like such a bad idea. My poetry was going nowhere other than my ability to mimic some of Eliot's lines. In a tiny quadrant of my heart the urbane staccato images and sounds of the 'The Waste Land' and seriocomic mocking of Profrock had found an uncertain shelf.

At the audition I was asked to do a series of bizarre improvisations.

Martin Delano, the director, was tall and lean, black hair graying on both sides pushed to one side away from his wide pale brow. His brown eyes were warm and intense. He reminded of Francoise Truffaut.

He spelled out my name on a clipboard saying out each letter out loud then after a brief welcome asked me to pretend to sit on an imaginary chair. This was followed by a request to eat an imaginary apple. Pause. Ok, now imagine being born. I fell to the floor and wiggled in a fetal position like an over-grown caterpillar.

—Next I want you to be electricity. Show me what it looks like. How does it move? Feel. Does it have a sound?

Each suggestion was followed by the same phrase 'take your time but don't take forever.'

No instructions or context. Just act. No questions please.

The audition was shocking in its simplicity and at the same time it made me feel exposed. I wondered how much of a fool I was making of myself. What was I revealing about myself?

I had expected a script. Lines to read. Instead here I was in a dull square room; above me heavy black stage lights on a silver bar below the ceiling. No theatre seats, no stage. Thin green industrial carpet, black walls, Martin leaning against the wall watching and smoking a cigarette.

—I am posting a list on the door outside. He pointed to the door.

—If your name is on the list, you are in the play. If you do not wish to be in the play, let me know ASAP. The actor's list will be up on Friday. See you at the party.

Martin did not mention the name of the play nor any character I might play.

I left feeling uncertain after the audition. What was I trying to do? What was I getting myself mixed up in? Pretend to be born again? I had the gnawing feeling I was on uncertain ground, slipped on a banana peel, and was falling down the rabbit hole.

Monica's apartment was at the end of the street in an old red brick apartment block with screened wooden balconies up the side. I parked on the next side street, and I guessed the place must be packed. I wasn't wrong. People were everywhere: some were squeezed on the couch. Another group stood talking, drinks in one hand, and cigarettes in the other. Still another cluster was sitting on the floor in a small circle playing back-gammon. In the kitchen two girls and one young man were talking so loud it seemed like yelling. They stopped to look at me for a moment and then ignored me. I thought they were high. Above the general dim, the Rolling Stones.

The kitchen table was covered with empty glasses, beer bottles, and half empty bottles of wine, vodka, and whiskey. A lonely blue plastic bowl full of melted ice sat at the center of it all. Beside it another bowl red with bits of potato chips at the bottom.

The entire apartment buzzed like an over-active beehive.

The large contingent of adults was a surprise. They were smoking pot. Their eyes squinted as they inhaled followed by a soft cough. It turned out they were some of Monica's professors.

One was an older gentleman with thick eyebrows, red/brown goatee and a rumpled brown turtleneck. He knew my sister Franca.

—Ah, your Franca's brother. Lucky girl to be working with Professor Zamponi and Dr. Clark. They are the best. Its part of her PhD course work I imagine.

—I think so. Yes, she knows it is a real feather in her cap to be working with them.

Standing beside him was an exotic looking couple. The man was significantly older than the young woman. Her face was oval and fine boned with high cheekbones, dark eyes. Their clothes marked them as European. They appeared relaxed by the surroundings as if they were the hosts.

—We are from Italy. My name is Gerard Luca, visiting Drama professor.

—Nino Ponte, student.

—Yes, of course a student. He smiled. You know the host well I understand.

—You mean Monica? I just met her.

My eyes scanned the room. Out of the corner of my eye I noticed her looking me over. She caught my glance and gave a thin Mona Lisa smile.

She looked both bohemian and feminine: leather jacket and underneath a ribbed black turtle neck sweater that curved over her breasts. Short grey skirt and black sheer nylons, flat sensible loafers. Her eyes were dark and large. She wore bright red lipstick. Her blonde hair fell like a curtain on both sides of her face. I thought of Franca for a split second when she straitened her hair.

Gerard stood aloof beside her like a tall stylish plantation owner. He was wearing a dark suit jacket and black and white stripped shirt. His black hair was grey at the temples and fell over his ears. I felt I had met him once before.

I went back into the kitchen for another beer. When I came back they were gone.

* * *

I got a part in the play. I knew no one in the cast. We soon started rehearsing. I was anxious about what we were doing. Part of the problem was there was no script. For the first month all we did was use our bodies as 'metaphors'. We were asked to make different sounds with our voices, move our bodies. It all seemed strange. I was confused and felt naked and exposed after each rehearsal. I wanted a script. A character to hide behind and not to have to explore my fear and loneliness, my confusion.

About a month before opening night Gerard and I met by accident. It was after Thanksgiving. The fall air felt heavy and thick, grass was brown. Leaves had burned yellow in one quick burst then fell into dull lifeless piles on the streets. Days were shorter, the dark asserted itself over everything, and the city streets were transformed by mysterious street light, shadows, and soft greys.

I was going up the stairs near the student bookstore and he was on his way down. We could not help meeting. Still, it felt as he had appeared out of the shadows, an unknown figure in an Escher painting.

—Nino, a pleasure. How are you? You left the party before saying good-bye.

I was feeling over-worked. The combination of rehearsals and courses was wearing me down. The long bus rides back to my apartment an exhausting journey past a dead zone of strip-malls, apartments, and dead beat hotels.

—I am fine thanks. How are you?

—Fine, fine. Why don't the three of us have dinner. Italians together in a foreign land. Here is my card. Call me.

He left and went down the stairs without waiting for my response. At the bottom of the stairs he turned and called up to me like a medieval troubadour to his lady in the tower. I also thought of the Rabbit from Alice in Wonderland dashing off after announcing he was late.

—Nino, nothing to worry about. Call. I will pay.

I wondered if his curiosity about me was based on a vulnerability which he wished to exploit. Did he see in me, as I sometimes thought, the raw materials of an artist?

Gerard was at ease in his own skin, urbane and confident. There was a sly grace about him. Then there was his shy pretty girl-friend. She seemed in sync with Gerard's arrogance. But, what was I seeking? The redemption of art?

* * *

We were finally given a script, Jean-Claude Van Itallie's play *The Serpent*.

The play revealed itself to be as strange as the rehearsals and unknowingly we had been vessels carrying and rehearsing a ceremony known as a play. Martin had deliberately kept us in the dark as we groped towards the play's basic question. What is the origin of evil? The action moved back to the primordial soup, Eden, fragmented voices, and then on to to another mythic event, each event in the play dissolving into the next until we arrived at the shooting of J.F.K.

We never left the stage, which was a bare open area surrounded by chairs. We simply transformed into something or someone else. 'The Serpent' was cutting edge avant-garde theater freshly minted four years earlier in the U.S. but none of us knew it and in the end it did not matter. Van Itallie was returning us the original garden.

The play opened for five nights, Tuesday through to Saturday, and it got good reviews. I was mentioned for my energetic performance. The reviewer missed my sullen sadness I thought obvious to everyone. Everyone knows unhappiness makes a good actor.

An after party was planned at the Montcalm Hotel after our last performance. My fellow actors were all Theater students and knew each other from shared classes.

I felt apart. I was not a full time theatre student. Plus, my aloofness, which in reality was a way of hiding my secret, had prevented me from making friends with the cast.

The weather suddenly changed again the day of our last show; it was cold and snow fell the entire day making the world look bright and clean. Solitary trees stood stark and empty against the sky.

She showed up at the last performance. I had not called about dinner. She was waiting for me by the stairs at University College in a navy-blue pea jacket and jeans, purse dangling in one arm, smoking, blonde hair up in a ponytail

—Ciao Nino. I stopped to tell you I liked the show, strange but I liked it. Your voice in the play is shocking. She smiled.

—Thanks. It is a strange play. Thanks for coming out. I didn't expect to see much of you. How are you?

—I am fine, fine. I get headaches from smoking too much.

—Is Gerard here?

—He is in Florence to see his mother. She is ill. So he says. I think he is visiting a woman he knows there. She shrugged.

She then pointed to a fresh Gitane cigarette. —Do you have any fire? then giggled.

We both lit up and walked to her car. The wind was blowing snow at fierce angles. Small snow drifts had formed on the sidewalks and streets. The snow swirled and spun in front of the car headlights in a mad arabesque dance. We sat in silence knowing we were going to sleep with each other again. The only sound was from the wind outside.

The radio announced that an unexpected Colorado Clipper had descended on the city. It advised to stay off the streets. It announced there had been a car accident with a snow-plow on the bridge that crossed over to my apartment on Broadway.

She turned her orange Volkswagen bug around a few blocks before we reached the Mid-Town Bridge and headed back towards the Pulmer Apartments on Wardlaw Street where she and Gerard lived.

We could not enter the parking lot behind the apartment block. The snow had blown thick drifts across the back lane and her car lacked enough weight to drive through the snow. She backed up and got stuck. I had to get out and push. She finally got some traction and spun around the corner and parked in the empty loading zone in front of her apartment building. My face, fingers, and toes were frozen from the effort.

She leaped out of the car:

—Lets go!

We made a mad dash up the long flight of stairs towards the apartment block doors trying to outrun the wind and snow. We stopped in the vestibule to catch our breath. Small white trails of breath rose above our mouths. My coat and jeans were encrusted with snow. She smiled her familiar smile and brushed the snow off.

She left me in the living room to put on a pot of coffee and use the bathroom. I sat on the couch thawing out my hands in the living room. The place was artistic, or if you like decorated in a modern graduate student style. It looked makeshift and European all at the same time. A bookshelf made of red planks and grey cinder blocks ran under the window facing the street and ended near a curved brown half rusted radiator. At each end of the top shelf was a plant in an orange Mediterranean vase with small blue spots. The bookshelf was filled with titles in English and Italian and some small ancient statues, Greek and Roman replicas, in random disorder between the shelves.

A fake ancient Greek Amphora stood by itself on an end table.

Stacks of newspapers were on the coffee table and some theater magazines along with two yellow legal size notepads with notes written in wide a distinctive cursive that reminded me of Franca. The Journal of Ancient Mediterranean Studies and its flat academic cover sat split on top of the newspapers. Two round black standup ashtrays stood on either end of a brown armchair with lipstick stained white filters. Against the wall a glass cabinet with bottles of foreign liquors and an open bottle each of scotch and brandy. On top of the cabinet two house plants one with one spidery vines that fell down the side. A tall brass lamp with a four-cornered white lampshade near the couch glowed a soft yellow erotic light. On the wall behind the lamp a red, yellow, and orange poster of an exhibition of the Fauve Painters at the Museum d' Orsay. On the other wall an African mask and a colorful print by Kandinsky.

She reentered the room and put on some John Coltrane, the sax slow and deep followed by unexpected free-flowing rifts. She passed me the coffee cup and held my hand before letting go. Outside you could hear the wind.

She leaned forward and pressed her face against mine.

—Your hands are so cold...

Her lips brushed mine. Her mouth tasted of tobacco and sour coffee. She placed my cold hand on her middle and leaned herself into it and sighed. She smiled again. We undressed. She let out a hiss and a series of murmurs each one a little louder than the last. She felt me gasp and lifted her head on to my neck and embraced me hard. I came inside her.

—Yes, all of you she whispered and I felt myself lift into her for a moment.

We lay still, glued together my face in her neck and hair.

After she was on her stomach one arm tucked under her chin smoking, a round black shiny ashtray on the bed in front of her. I gazed down her spine; behind her on the wall her ass formed the shadow of two small curved hills.

—I thought you were shy. I guess I was wrong.

She flashed an impish smile. Her eyes caught the light. They seemed to sparkle.

—I am shy.

I was feeling dazed as if drugged and relaxed. I frowned and blushed.

—It's not a bad thing.

She flicked her cigarette over the ashtray inhaled deeply, and then released the smoke into the air above her.

—I am telling you I am shy. Even the damn play made me feel shy. But, I wanted to try something new. Explore. See if I would like it. Learn something about myself.

—Trust me you are a very good actor and a fast learner.

She smiled and savored the double entendre.

—Not exactly. Tired of my old self, formulated, sprawling on a pin.

—Miss our, I mean, my parents.

She reached and touched my brow.

—T.S. Eliot, nice. We are on a quest. Will you fight for my garter? Quests usually end well for the hero but first there is lots of hardship and suffering. You must be strong and cunning. Am I your muse?

—I am trying to figure that out.

—Be shrewd. Mediterranean people admire a shrewd operator, a man of wits, a silver tongue. Actually, we all admire shrewdness.

I thought of my father. He certainly tried to be a man of wits and loquacious argument.

—It's the desire for purity that makes a mess out of everything. Put it out of your mind.

She put her hand under the blanket.

—Now where is your sword? Did you know your ego gets stronger every time you come?

I did not have an answer for her not that she seriously expected one from me. I sensed she knew I was not experienced as her in the matters of the flesh, or the heart for that matter.

We fell asleep with the wind outside howling and hitting the windows.

I dreamed her and I were lost in a snowy forest. Tall dark spruce trees and snow fell slow and gentle, as if in a snow globe. The wind in abrupt loud gusts swept through the dense branches of the evergreens. We found shelter in a small space under a large Evergreen tree. I felt myself go deep into her.

I awoke and stared at the ceiling and tried focusing on what would happen if Gerard discovered our tryst. It occurred to me that maybe I had been conscripted into a complicated game, enrolled in a jealous payback script sprung from her fresh wide forehead. What was next? The situation seemed sophisticated, worldly. What was she was hiding? Running from?

* * *

We have discovered an old well. It is on an ancient side street in Catamaran di Chianti in Tuscany. There are three levels to the well: Medieval, Roman, and Etruscan. We have found artifacts from all three periods. The bronze, silver, and ceramics pots from the Etruscan period are the most exciting. There are some Roman votive coins and wine seeds. It will add to our understanding of the history of wine in the region during Roman and Etruscan times. We are all excited by the finds. It should add a few chapters to my PhD.

Don't ask what the ticket cost. It's your Christmas present. You will love Perugia, a pretty hilltop town north of Rome. I booked rooms for us at the Priori Hotel off Corso Vannucci. There is a great view of the valley and Assisi in the distance. Let's go there for Midnight Mass.

Florence and Rome are way too expensive. See you soon.

Love always,

Franca

Gerard had called a week before on a Sunday night to say he would be late coming home. We were in bed when he called. They spoke in Italian; I could hear his voice sounding remote and tinny. She pushed my face away from the phone and mouthed the word private.

I responded by playfully pulling one of her breasts out from her nightshirt and encasing half her breast in my mouth. She gasped and pushed me off with her free hand.

—That was not smart. He heard me gasp. I told him the tree branches outside the apartment had scratched against the window and scared me. There is no need for you to be jealous. Accept what we have now.

I was not good at being the cool self-possessed lover. Her rebuke made me feel childish and unsophisticated. I resented her detachment about us. I left the apartment without saying goodbye.

The bus shuttle from Fiumcino airport to the train station took about forty-five minutes but not before we passed a series of arid apartment complexes in a dusty scrub landscape outside of Rome. In the distance there were the ancient dark mountains against a blue sky; ruins dotted the landscape, old fallen walls and aqueducts looked abandoned and forlorn. We entered the city via the old Aurelian walls and past the Pyramid of Cestius near the Porta San Paolo.

Here the magical jumble that is Rome took over; old and white pock marked columns from antiquity stood embedded beside dark sixteenth century windows and walls, remote baroque churches glared at eighteenth century paving stones. Big and small fountains splashed in the streets. Drowsy palm trees jutted out from behind high courtyard walls. Laundry on balconies and everywhere patches of soft buttery light – the kind you only see on a Roman winter morning – hit the old brown, red, and yellow and graffiti sprayed walls

The bus headed up up Via Nazionale, towards the Termini train station. Traffic slowed just long enough for me to make out the sweep of Gerard's hair to the left of his brow and the distinguished grey on each side and his arrogant uplifted nose. He was impeccably dressed, much like the last time I saw him, only this time he was wearing a black wool overcoat and a rich coloured scarf and gold tie. Franca, my sister, was on his arm leaning towards his face and dressed in a black navy pea-jacket, collar up, partially covering her cheeks. She wore an elegant gold and yellow scarf. Her blonde hair was tied up in a classic French bun but a few long bangs hung curved on each of her face. She held a small paperback – or was it a guidebook – under her other arm. They looked happy together.

I thought of jumping off the bus and surprising them but when I took a second look I became confused and fell into a state of disbelief and indecision. Before I could decide what to do the bus accelerated and at that very moment they turned on to a side street and vanished.

I got off the bus and took a moment to look down Via Nazionale before heading off to the train station. The marble stairs of the war memorial at the bottom of the street floated in the distance under a bright blue sunlit sky. What I had just seen? Was my exhaustion causing me to see things? Was it the sudden richness of Rome? The fountain in the Piazza Della Repubblica splashed softly in a quiet realistic way.

The Termini train station at mid-morning five days before Christmas resembled an over-turned anthill. People were rushing to and from the station from all directions in all manner of shape, size, and dress. Some sat in the station caffe and enjoyed a morning cappuccino, others knocked back an espresso in two quick gulps.

I ordered an espresso, drained it quickly, and bought a fresh pack of cigarettes – Italian – and a new lighter before heading over to·one of the ticket gates. I felt haunted. It occurred to me that Martin looked like Gerard.

A train left for Perugia on time an hour later. I had to change trains twice. This involved a heart-stopping dash from one side of the train platform to another by way of a tunnel under the station.

The last change took place at Foligno, a half-hour before we reached Perugia. The people on the train were in a festive mood carrying Christmas packages even though some were standing. All the seats were taken.

She, however, had managed to sit down beside me. She looked exhausted and asked me to make room for her small black carry-on luggage.

Her eyes were alert and although she was tired she took great delight in nimbly plucking a cigarette from my fresh pack. She stood with one hand under her elbow holding up the other arm with the cigarette between her fingers waiting for me to give her a light. Her navy blue winter coat was strung over her shoulders. Underneath her coat tight blue jeans and a maroon V neck sweater. A mixed orange, yellow, and gold scarf lay loosely knotted around her neck. I guessed her to be my sister Franca's age somewhere between twenty-eight and thirty.

—Ah, Muratti my favorite. So what brings you to Perugia at Christmas? Its too early for the new semester at the university.

—I am here to meet my sister for the holidays. She is working on an archaeological site in a village near Florence.

—You left your parents behind at Christmas? Shame on you!

—My parents are dead. Car accident.

—Oh, I'm sorry.

She turned embarrassed and stared out the window at the landscape as it flickered past in a blur of red unplowed fields and neat green gardens, farmhouses, fences, and brown limestone huts.

She paused and inhaled deeply and blew smoke up towards the top of the train window.

—Oh, Dio…I travel too much. It makes me so tired.

A weary melancholy descended over her and then disappeared.

—I would like to meet your sister. You think we can meet before I go to Florence for Christmas. Lunch, a drink, and a few cigarettes? Come to Bar Turreno behind the Cathedral. It's a socialist bar. You can meet my friends. Ok?

It was late afternoon when I finally checked into the Priori

Hotel. She was right about the view from the hotel: ancient stone houses organically followed the rise and fall and curves of the hill, well-ordered fields stretched far as the monastery of Assisi. Dark blue mountains sat in a blurred hazy outline far in the distance. Large island sized clouds hung low and grey with open bits of blue between them.

I walked down Corso Vanucci past the crenellated Palazzo dei Priori and its thick medieval doors towards the Cathedral and the piazza and its fountain from the 13th century. Men and women of all ages were out for a stroll elegantly dressed before dinner. Some had stopped for a quick aperitif and chat; groups of students moved like schools of fish eating pizza slices and joked with each other, Older gentlemen in winter wool coat and scarf sat in the outdoor cafes smoking and talking, newspaper tucked under one arm.

Franca had bathed and was waiting for me when I returned from my walk. Her thick blonde curly hair on the pillow looked like woven sunlight. One foot was tucked under a bare thigh.

—Welcome back, she smiled.

I fell into her arms relived we had at last a few days together to once again try and shed our impossible grief away from Gerard and the eyes of the world.

Writers and Lovers

I fell or perhaps better stumbled towards the future like a tumbling circus clown. The summer, well, it was the summer prelude before the fall and is it not fair to say a fall was also a start? And now I have come back, come back to what was once a broken town to what is now a place puffy with pride and the dead. Where to start? I could start with my dead wife. Yes, yes, there were times we never loved each other much and regret poured out to strangers in the middle of the night in far and distance cities where no else knew me or her for that matter and it was as simple as hitching up a seat-belt and talking to a total stranger on a ride fueled by booze and the vague hope something promiscuous would come of my morose behavior. Still, I say, my finger jauntily pointed at the ceiling, eyeing the jury, in this case the thirty something blonde twirling her drink half in amusement, half in horror at my discourse on the metaphysics of marital love and no doubt questioning herself why she made eye-contact with me in the first place.

Apart from my well-polished loafers – black with a saw tooth patch of leather for style and faux lace ups – I am also not a bad looking roué. Notable full grey temples, the rest salt and pepper swept to one-side in a full wave, broad firm shoulders – I continue to go to the gym – and I have a smile that wrinkles the corner of my eyes like a man in a cigarette ad and my eyes do twinkle in the dim-light of a hotel bar when amused and my heart pounds like a that of a teenager if lust slips into my blood-stream after I catch a glimpse of her black bra strap or note the way her breasts are at at home in a familiar grip just below her décolleté.

Yes, my wife and I argued and yes we came together like mercury after shattering in a mad heedless way and we did this repeatedly over thirty years until our own special kind of love madness redefined Tolstoy's quip about how happy families are all alike.

I am here back at the scene of the crime so to speak – why, oh why, do we always return – after a long absence, invited no less by the Writers' Circle of Canada, a kind of Shrine circus for egg-heads minus the Fez hats and the small bicycles and scooters. Instead, there are the over-sized egos and matching sweaters, the usual coterie of suburban men and women angry and pious who teach in comfortable universities and are published by friends, and many hapless but not necessarily happy bovine writers who work at scheming their way to the top by playing victim. Take as typical Jo-Anne Basinet or was it Basel net, nut, whatever. First, she does in fact have a round fleshy face and eyes like a cow and a thick body that managed to attract a husband. I know little of her literary career and apart from her repeated attempts to become a Country & Western singer – she howled out her 'songs' in the imitation of who knows what, a dog? (see what Leonard Cohen's success has wrought!) – while she pursued one after another writer-in-residence jobs across Canada and peddling false modesty at being invited to read in support of her kind at yet another obscure and bland literary gathering. Her comrade-in-arms, Michelle Cartier, a defrocked thin-skinned professor who imagined herself to be the next Willa Cather praising the wonders of canoeing on a cold lake in summer with someone who has a lovely soul. Oh, the wonders indeed but I digress, the Writers' Circle did ask me – to my shock and surprise, as Lord Mountbatten was fond of saying to no one in particular – to read from one of my travel books and sit in on a panel discussion oddly called 'Why travel books in the 21ˢᵗ century.' Why not was my first response and ignored the invitation. But my dear publisher – the bastard is the one who arranged it all – more or less said the following:

—Henry this is prime real estate. Go and sell books. Be an ambassador for your work. Besides your latest is out at the same time as the conference. Rumour has it they may even give you an award for all your work.

—Honestly, Nino, I don't want to go. Never been a member and never will be. The worse company for a writer is another writer. There is never enough oxygen in the room for both of them. I can't stand their hopeless beaten dog look – they all look like they have not bought a decent pair of clothes since 1980 – and the morbid tones and their pithy irony serving to defend some imaginary political or social line in the sand. Have you ever watched them eat? It matches that horrible eating and drinking scene in *Ulysses*. Hobos is what my poor dead Helena used to call their comportment. Now tell the truth is this why you waited until June to release my book. And in Winnipeg no less!

—Henry, Winnipeg is your hometown. What better place to launch your tenth book? A book out every two years for the last twenty years should be feted.

—I am not in the feting mood.

—All the more reason for you to go. Mingle with your many admirers. They are paying for the flight for God-sake. Who does that anymore?

—Well, you certainly don't. I'll go if you pay for my daughter's ticket. I refuse to go back home without my daughter. Mingle by the way rhymes with thimble and one half full is how much I think of my many admirers.

The real reason I agreed – apart for a chance to have a few dinners and a walkabout with my daughter – is I wanted to go back and visit the places Helena and I haunted before we ended up in Toronto at 22 Constance Street in a three story dark-wooded Edwardian home – the rooms set pieces for what in fact became Edwardian melodrama on more than one occasion when for example I came through the door blood and lip-stick stained as if I had attended a dinner hosted by Sephora vampires. There were indeed some high-ended 'horas', dancers, and an unexplainable flying of fists. Russian and Italian strip-club owners are a bad mix, a meeting of free-flowing methane and a propane lighter.

* * *

Colin and Vickie Fitzgerald were brother and sister and lived together after Vickie returned from a failed attempt at a PhD in architecture. I had returned to Winnipeg from Italy after a year of too much beauty and failure in Italy. I met Vickie first and became reacquainted with Colin later.

I originally knew Colin in a vague way as one of many faces you passed by in a high school hallway during the blank dull days of winter and in summer recall seeing him often standing around in the school parking lot with his pals, an obvious pack of smiling and smoking prank orientated Grade Elevens. He then disappears from view and reappears still at a distance in the university Arts Lounge wearing an Indian scarf and jeans tucked into Frye boots which added to his height. He was in Fine Arts and performed very much like a handsome rogue pirate/poet by injecting snatches of Bob Dylan songs ('there must be some kind of way out here said the joker to the thief') between the inhaling of a cigarette and a zip of coffee from a white Styrofoam cup. There was usually a good-looking girl or two near, pleased to be plant-like under the glow of his sunny smile. His ability to attract women or at least be around them in various shapes, size, and looks was impressive.

Then came the return of Vickie and I from different points on the map only to land in Winnipeg a month apart and by some mysterious cause and effect – the outline of which only becomes recognizable once everything has fallen apart and you are forced to look for a beginning only because you only know the ending with any clarity – we met.

None of this is of any interest to my daughter, at least that is what I presumed. She is a sensible young woman like her mother and her ability to tolerate ambiguity is low accompanied by a dislike of surprise except perhaps in a book. I learned all of this early when we set off to fulfill my promise to take her to Paris and Rome for her thirteenth birthday and in the process write my third travel book. My book on train travel along the northern coasts of South America had done well and was therefore flush with cash for a change. It had been a calculated move to write about train travel after watching the enduring success of other train travel writers. There was also the bit of money that had remained from the sale of the last piece of my Dad's farmland near Portage La Prairie. Everything nicely dove-tailed together, her birthday and new money, and away we went to see the world. My plan was to drive down the Champs-Elysees in a sports car with the wind in our hair. I was uncertain whether it would be possible to have a glass each in our hand and as we approached one of the largest roundabouts in the world – The Arc de Triomphe – toast Paris, her birthday, and our good fortune.

Little did we know disaster was waiting quiet and still in

the beautiful body of Helena. To this day whenever any kind of success draws near a deep fearful anxiety falls over me anticipating some dreadful fall. While Celeste and I were out and about enjoying the squeaky clean streets, shops, and cafes of Paris (the local Parisians an exception) Helena was having her breasts pressed and photographed and sure enough on the second last day of our visit aboard there was a message to call home when we retuned from the unexpected wet streets of St. Michel in the evening.

I can't even write the word, in fact, I refuse to in the shamanistic belief that by not naming it does not exist. The evening and the flight home the next day were a blur. We both fell silent and tried unsuccessfully to distract each other and pretend we were returning home better, nicer, and happier and smarter, that travel in some unexplainable way 'broadens experience,' a falsehood and cliché if there ever was one.

So here I am twenty years later Celeste is 33, Helena gone for the past nineteen, and I have crossed the frontier known as sixty-five.

Travel is like writing: it involves a reckoning and openness, requires memory, (notebooks and a good eye are welcome) and concludes with an encounter both inside and out that may or not make sense. It angers me that the majority of readers couldn't careless how you came to write your damn precious book in the first place.

In the beginning I was reluctant to put pen to paper. It did not seem like a manly thing to do but as I told her stories of my year in Italy after our many post-coital embraces, smoke above us in a thin blue veil, her smile wide and generous, Vickie convinced me I had a story to tell.

—Henry you are so funny, sad, and romantic. Sometimes even pathetic. You should write it all down just as you told me. I love how you can imitate people's voices.

I had just told her another story using a fake French accent. This time it was the one about my disastrous meeting with Jenna – a Franco-German woman who possessed a combustion engine for a heart – one afternoon in the the empty long-shadowed Boboli Gardens behind the Pitti Palace in Florence on a cold day in the middle of January. Why did I not try and kiss her she complained, lips pursued and puckered like a large Chinese goldfish as she hissed the H and rolled the I in my name in French. We stood like two chess pieces toe to toe in the crisp cold winter sunlight staring into each others eyes as tobacco smoke and our hot breath frosted and fogged and streamed from our mouths like badly formed thought bubbles in an adult comic book called Hotel.

—Honest and cross my – ohm, mm – never mind – you are good. A natural story-teller.

—Sex has clouded your judgment. By the way when do I get to meet your brother Colin?

I had not yet told Vickie that I remembered her brother in high school and later would watch him perform in the university Arts lounge usually in the late afternoon after most classes were done and sun poured through the tall windows highlighting the tattered couches, arm-chairs, and the stout black silver rimmed ash-trays over-flowing with butts and the odd coffee-cup and wrapper. I idly wondered what he would think when he found out Vickie and I were an item as they used to say back then or if he would even remember me. It was a small private school for boys with some three hundred students tops and although everyone pretty much had their own little clique to hang out with you did tend to know the most of the guys a grade head and below you.

So, it was likely he had some mental image of me and no doubt some opinion based on the residuals of my past public as a teenager. But, now we were no longer young and he had already become a darling of the Canadian art world whereas I continued to flounder – no more like dripped out – one cloudy olive oil drop at a long time – my book. Vickie's various oral encouragements aside I was in a suppressed panic that I would never find a publisher or audience about neglected Umbria and Calabria. I admired Eric Newby's *A Small Place in Italy* and his precise clear way of looking and writing about landscape and his ability to capture the essence of the local contadini, farmer's, characters on the border of Liguria and Tuscany, his droll humour, and his easy ability to connect with the locals was admirable.

I was, in contrast, quarrelsome and uncertain how to reconcile my different images and impressions of Italy. My Italian was not strong and it was therefore tough to get past the surface of things in conversation and tough not to believe that every so often I was being had in a café or when, say, asking about the local olive trees, or poking around in an antique shop.

Unlike Newby, I did not trust the Italians much. Then there was the difference between the cultural landscapes in Umbria and Calabria, a study in contrasts if there ever was one, as well as the ancient division or uneasy political marriage/alliance between Northern and Southern Italy, vast and various and beyond the original use of the phrase by the Italian poet Montale to describe the ever churning sea. And there was the crowd that was Jenna, her capriciousness, her moody sulks, rage about love found and lost, her sudden disappearance only to reappear a day later smelling of sea salt, stale cigarettes, and maraschino cherries, her hair the shape of a tumbleweed. All of this confusion and drama you could say made writing my first book a bit like trying to put together a jig-saw puzzle on an open raft in a storm. But to give Vickie her due, she pushed past my self-doubt and my curious antipathy that co-existed with my desire to put pen to paper.

Colin returned from Venice and moved back in with Vickie on Thursday two days before his next art show in the Exchange. I packed my worn out toothbrush and a few of my things the night before and moved back to my apartment on Wardlaw Avenue. The next day Vickie phoned to tell me she had scheduled a Saturday morning get together before Colin's art opening Saturday night. But, then something came up at the gallery – a big room on the third floor of a former warehouse with old floorboards redone and still visible rusty nails, white washed walls, and track lighting – so instead it was the three of us, Colin's girl-friend, Vickie and I at breakfast.

Vickie and I were sitting at the end of a row tables when she arrived; Vickie waved and she waved back walking towards us and our eyes locked. Although I have never been one to believe in love at first sight and all that *Romeo and Juliette* jazz, a strange and unexpected feeling came over me that must have had some striking similarity to Saul being struck on the road to Damascus minus the Lord's voice and flash of light or the three days of blindness. Mind, we could not stop looking at each other – a type of blindness – over our sausages & eggs over-easy and eating toast and marmalade suddenly seemed suggestive. Later that evening at the gallery we continued to look at each other whenever possible. It was what the Japanese call **Koi no Yokan**: the sense you have on meeting another person for the first time that you will fall in love with them. She looked stunning in a simple navy blue and small white polka-doted summer dress out of which came a pair of thin arms and legs. She was not a tall woman, one and a half meters give or take a few with big brown impish eyes, reddish brown hair with long girlish pleats on both sides, sensual lips, the bottom lip especially plump and full, and a mischief smile. She walked or floated from one art piece to the next in a casual, light, and unhurried way turning ever so often to see where I was standing in the room and our eyes would meet. We could not stop looking at each other. It was our version of the Jean Luc Godard meets Anna Karina moment. Not wishing to be more obvious than I already was I gave Helena a copy of my first book with a small note inside asking her to meet me at midnight at a Russian run café on Sherbrook Street that simply called itself café. The book, alas, was dedicated to Vickie Fitzgerald. I hoped she would overlook this small fact.

She showed up late and smiled and told me she had no where to stay and that all her things were at Colin and Vickie's apartment on Westminster Avenue. Before she left the Blow Up Gallery Colin demanded to know what I had written in the book. She said no and there was a bit of a struggle and at first he was furious and he then followed her down three flights of stairs to the waiting cab below howling and begging her to stay and and saying where did she think she was going Winnipeg was not her hometown.

—There Celeste, see where it says Deli? That is where the cafe used to be. It was a little place run by Russian Jews, no more than eight tables. I hated the lighting. Way too bright. But they made the best Pelmeni, a kind of Russian dumpling, and they made Napoleon Torte, a cake made by stacking up thin layers of pastry and between the layers was a thick vanilla-apricot custard filling. My God it was good. Your mother and I loved the place.

City planning, Architecture, and Roxana's aesthetics: An erotic story in the form of a short French film

At some point I came to the realization that one of the supreme pleasures in life is to be in a beautiful city with a beautiful woman. They both have a grid of pleasure, size, curve, shape, and texture created by design, happy accident, and unexplainable and disorganized homage to the present and past (I am thinking about how cities are built and how women dress) interacting to create a symmetry of visual delight or blight and careful randomness also known as casual.

* * *

Roxana has large pretty eyes, dark medium length hair. White pale skin. Big nipples. She paid $10,000 for her 36B tits and cried when she first saw them.

She showed the surgeon pictures of what she wanted but he still did not do them right. She now has plans to have them re-done and made bigger.

* * *

She loves to run. Used to play mid-field on a soccer team. Later, she played semi-pro soccer in Perugia.

Running makes her focused. She now uses the trend-mill. Reading makes her cry.

* * *

She giggles and laughs to herself as she talks to me. She wants to be a writer.

Her mother encourages her to write. She likes people.

* * *

She thinks I am kind.

* * *

Roxana has a thing for numbers. Certain numbers are always coming into her life.

The number 222 for example. She ate a pizza at Café 222, her apt. number is 222, she was born February 22 and she is 42. Her soccer jersey was number 32.

She thinks she has the gift of prophecy. The future is there for everyone to see she says.

* * *

She tells me her stomach and pussy hurt today. She did Greek once and started bleeding 'just like that.'

* * *

She does not like it when a man puts his fingers inside her, 'only on the outside.'

* * *

I like how she asks "you like doggie style"? I enjoy looking at her, holding her soft round cheeks. She seems matter of fact about the whole thing. Bored.

* * *

I read somewhere that the finished poem is present even before it is edited and finally written. Michelangelo said something similar about releasing the already present sculpture from a block of marble. Roxana's idea of prophecy: The future is a kind of waiting room for the present to happen, she says.

* * *

"Abstraction exhausts and kills. Its an impasse. Let's be on guard against falling into the subsoil of the unconscious. To paint I have to have a living model in front of me." A. Modigliani. He was a sculptor before taking up painting because the dust was so hard on his damaged lungs.

The triumph of the still image, the movement of language, the mind's natural ability to create dreams. The made image of the painter filtered through the rational sensuous mind versus the natural made images of dream by the mind.

Both are natural processes.

Cubism and abstract art a dead-end.

City-planning can never be surreal.

Seduction involves all the five senses and explains why surrealism, in spite of its best efforts, can never be erotic.

This also explains why rational city-planning (think of the Romans) enhances the erotic inherit in a city's design.

* * *

Roxana's way of seeing leads one to believe that surrealism is in fact bad memory combined with dream imagery, garnished with clues that suggest both sense and nonsense.

* * *

The curves of the river here and some women have shaped city streets and their names. There is a straight line West from here, another line runs South there, while still others are built close to the river banks, curved and meandering. Wellington Crescent follows the curves and accidental meandering of water lay down thousands of years ago.

There are at least five streets in the North-End named after women: Nora, Flora, Gertie, Harriet, Ellen and Francis to name a few, suggested by city-planners and councillors at the turn of the century more or less.

* * *

Architecture is the ultimate erotic act. When carried to excess it reveals both reason and a sensual experience of space simultaneously.

As for Roxana, she never returned to the city.

The Poets

It was October. She wore tight jeans, a shirtless blue V-neck sweater, brown penny loafers, her hair cascaded in thick abundant waves, a Paris fall look. Jenna at the Caffe Rivoire. To tell this story I must go back in time and try and visit an old self or at the least a self that was moving towards an idea or what it wanted to be. At times the idea was indistinct.

I am now old enough to reject my old ideas and rationalizations although still not certain that what I have learned or if what I am about to tell you will be of any interest or use.

The lawns outside are solid green. Tress full of different shapes and sizes stand silent and still. Sunlight is white under a blue-sky streaked with a thin transparent cloud cover. The flowers in the garden are in full bloom. Large heavy purple begonias bend, orange lilies stand straight, small discreet bunches of white daisies soak up the sun. The cement sidewalks tilted and uneven up close appear straight as they run endlessly towards the far end of the street. The wide flat streets are made of asphalt and curve around the corner past a row of apartment blocks. Traffic moves harmoniously back and forth on Corydon Avenue in the bright July sunlight.

Cars and their invisible pistons move north and south in an endless motion. At a glance the small world outside my window is busy and orderly.

I think of her body. The small calf muscle behind her leg that rises and then slopes downwards toward her ankle. Her hand griping the sheet. The way her stomach rippled like a blanket when she pulled up her skirt. Her plump small breasts barely contained in her bra just before she buckled it up. The sudden curve along her back just below the shoulder at the end of summer when she reached with her other hand. Her purple wool winter socks lying side by side, split at the heel like a large plum.

The arch of her back when she lifted her hips. After a marine scent and the taste of espresso and tobacco on her lips. The tiny wrinkles at the end of her round smooth cheeks when she turned away from my view. The wrinkles in the corner of her eyes when she laughed. Jenna.

The orderly world outside my window is not what it seems, a basic principle probably dating as far back to the time when we stood up on our hind legs and gazed over the tall grass into the distance.

I write this to tell to you that at this distance what remains are impressions, images, and uncertain dates and times. Facts cannot always be the only basis for what we know or believe. Nor is it a simple matter of writing everything down and you reading it. Reading creates an experience as much as reenacts or tells it. Memory is an editor.

At one time I was unable to admit I loved her. Now it seems like a useless thing to do and perhaps I say it to myself to identify the emptiness I feel. That is one experience…

I admire the clarity and elegant phrasing of good poets; the sudden crack of ice when you read a powerful fresh metaphor is an experience, a new way of seeing and thinking. Poetry can take us away for a moment from the everyday world of driving to and from work, shopping for groceries, washing dishes, annoyance at the racket a vacuum cleaner makes. Poetry can and does tie all of it together to a discreet self. Poetry is a way of knowing we often ignore or quickly allow to pass over us like a brief splash of water on the face before we return to the business of arriving safely home. Poetry, like sensuality, feels impermanent and unsustainable, a moment or a series of moments that melt before they can be held in the imperfect container of the heart. Sadness sits inside the core of beauty. The beauty of a poem. Jenna. The story of Jenna and the divided poet. Aren't all poets divided?

* * *

We entered Florence for the first time on a drive up from Perugia. Wolfgang took the E35 around Lake Trasimeno early in the morning. We had descended from the Piazza Italia at the top of Perugia's center, the road down a series of switchbacks that resembled the indiscriminate and accidental swirls on a vanilla ice-cream. This did not help my hang-over. Then we headed north, driving along the long slow curve around the lake. The day and the lake were grey, but occasionally sunlight found its way out of the prison of thick slow moving clouds and fell on to the lake. The light sparkled and splintered off the small lake waves like the endpoints of Christmas lights. Or for a few minutes the sunlight sat on top of the water like a square shiny piece of moving white satin. Italy never ceased being beautiful even on a cloudy day.

The night before it was the four of us for dinner at Jenna's apartment. We were all strangers to each other yet there we were giving it a go at normal life. The conversation was constrained. I often did not know what the three of them said to each other in German and watched their faces to get some clue. We knew each other from the university except for Ingrid who met Jenna on the train in Bologna. She worked for a tour company out of Vienna and was on a work expedition. Jenna and her Austrian roommate Ingrid, had attempted to cook a kind of crepe ratatouille for Wolfgang and me but, the vegetables were undercooked and raw, the zucchini and green peppers crunched, the tomatoes watery, an overuse of onion did nothing but irritate. The whole dish tasted lifeless and bland – even in candle-light – and diluted yellow spots of olive-oil hovered over the entire simmering mess. The awful food lifted the conversation and our spirits. We bonded over the awfulness of it all. We dipped round pieces of bread into the mess laughing at the disaster in our plates and drank lots and lots of white wine to avoid the food. We smoked at first greedily between each sip of wine but eventually a languor fell over the table. The evening had started out slow and nervous, each of us reserved and uncertain of the other, but in the end Wolfgang and I were calling out for more wine under Jenna and Ingrid's window. We now were willing to exchange some cream filled pastries bought fresh from the bakery across the piazza from their apartment for wine. The reply was shriller laughter-it felt as if I was in one of Chaucer's Canterbury Tales – and a large empty two-liter bottle of wine was dropped towards us and the shutters closed with a thud. The bottle made a loud crash on the silent empty street. It was after midnight. The commotion and crash made me panic at the thought we had awaken the entire street. Wolfgang and I hastily vanished under the cover of the half-lit streets back to our respective apartments to avoid being found out as the culprits or intended victims by the locals. Unspoken desire denied.

Over dinner we had decided it would be fun to visit Florence. Ingrid at the last moment sleepily begged off, the very moment in fact Wolfgang showed up with his car.

We entered Florence just as the radio started to play the French pop song "A Man and A Woman," the "bababdadada" refrain and chorus perfectly mirroring in an uncanny and mischievous way late morning traffic. Cars honked or sped past us with causal intent, Vespa's darted in and out of narrow traffic lanes, "badabadadada…," a passenger on the backseat of a scooter flashed a peace sign and gave me a smile as she zipped by. Ancient and cracked dun-coloured walls, green shutters, low red brick-tiled rooftops, churches, arched door-ways, and signs for hotels, restaurants, and bars flickered by in slow motion as Wolfgang hunted for a parking spot.

The song also ironically mirrored the ambiguous roman-tic situation Jenna, Wolfgang, and I had created and now found ourselves stuck in. For almost the entire drive Wolfgang insisted on speaking German to Jenna and ignored me in the backseat. We both had been flirting with Jenna the night be-fore. I imagined once we reached Florence he hoped I would somehow disappear. Boozy born friendships between poets are seldom reliable.

The day was in flux. The city and the situation new to me but fitted what I thought represented European sophistication and free-spirited artistic freedom.

We parked at the far end of Borgo Pinti and Wolfgang's guide book-map lead us to the over-priced Caffé Rivoire on Piazza della Signoria over-looking the sensible and solid Palazzo Vecchio, and to the right the passionate intensity of the sculptures in the Loggia dei Lanzi. Jenna took a liking to Cellini's bronze *Perseus with the head of Medusa*, his strong lean muscular body, the bloody violence of the severed head in his upraised hand and body at Perseus's feet, a look of shock and disgust on his face. It confirmed what I knew of her con-trolled turbulent, witty and sensual poems. Her poems took amazing risks and succeeded. Her fierce intelligence took no prisoners. Her poems, like Florence itself, were full of beauti-ful opposites: the ancient and the shabby, glittering fashion-able shop-windows and small discreet artisan's hovels, playful sensuality and sad disappointment, elegant courtyards and dirty side-streets, the history of church architecture at a glance and the profane everywhere.

We spent some time together site-seeing around Il Duomo. Jenna dismissed it all, the church, baptistery, the crowds swirling around. She repeated more than once that what we saw was all kitsch. At some point we separated for a a few hours to explore on our own. Shortly after, I came across Jenna sitting alone smoking at a table in Gilli Caffé in Piazza della Repubblica.

Her head was tilted towards the book she was reading with her sunglasses on so it was impossible for her to notice me.

I noted the way she had organized her caffe table. Her red and white cigarette pack off to the side and her black square Zippo lighter neat and square on top. Her espresso was on a right angle in front of her and the small pitcher of water with glass just behind the espresso cup. She could have been posing for a portrait or waiting for someone.

I considered surprising her then hesitated and finally decided it was best to leave her alone. She looked like she did not want to be be disturbed. The elegance of the cafe and some kind of misplaced notion of gentlemanly behavior also held me in check. I turned back and crossed Ponte Vecchio and walked past the tourists clamoring in front of the Pitti Palace and headed instead towards the less visited Santo Spirito neighborhood singing under my breath 'like a bird on a wire, like a drunk in a midnight choir…'

I was angry at myself for being so passive and indecisive. I wanted a new self.

* * *

It was now the middle of December and I wondered if my move to Italy was such a good idea. I was not writing and when I did sit down to write my mind inevitably drifted away towards my last words, my last dinner, my last kiss, my last argument with Jenna. The relationship was distracting me away from myself and my work. Yet in the corner of my mind I thought it was all grist for the artistic mill. The drama could be used to make art and provide interior knowledge. The soul should flare, I thought.

Then there were all the big and small gestures Florence offered up. Everyday there were a series of casual and ancient images and feelings from the flawed beauty of the medieval streets and church frescoes to the ache felt inside a few bars of a bittersweet Italian love song that had drifted onto the street.

At night it was the neon signs on Via National, or the slow back and forth, pull and release of her dress over her round cheeks, streetlight glistening on the slate grey paving-stones after it rained. Of course, I was also annoyed by tourist buses disgorging yet another bus tour-this was now after all my Florence: the cigarette ash dangling from a half smoked cigarette on the lips of my new friend the old newspaper vendor, cool dark shadows on the pavement of some ancient arches from the side wall of a palazzo, the smell of fresh espresso and clatter of dishes and spoons on the bar counter, the washed out blue sky and changing light. I was captivated by it all and wanted it to belong to me.

But, I was exhausted by the sheer weight and accumulated beauty and elegance of it all, alienated by my struggle to find stable work. Florence mocks an outsider if you stay too long and the elegant shops cruel in their self-important sense of style and grace.

I wondered how long I could last. I wanted to leave for the

free and easy beaches of Greece and abandon the idle fantasy of living by my wits and writing, of holding Jenna, before my money ran out.

* * *

Polyglot letters eventually arrived, magnificent mischief.

Ciao Tomato!!,

Comment ca va? Sono ora in Sardegna. Come and visit moi. Beautiful mare, so blue. Wolfgang is now triste and so are you and me too. Come back tomato. Miss me? Enjoy moi! Truly, Wolfgang and I are always almost fini. I know you think I am a wild gatto. Fuck ton comportement makes me crazy. Why did you not kiss me in the Boboli gardens? Fuck money. I am honey. My nipples burn per te. C'est fou, l'amore c'est tout fou...

Je tien gross bras,
Jenna

Jenna could never write English well or Italian and she knew I could not read German. Her French, however, was impeccable. So, she wrote in all four languages in some kind of mad Molly Bloom Joycean stream-of-consciousness way.

I had left her and Florence and Italy and returned to Canada.

There had been no grand reckoning, no dramatic ending full of tears, shouting, and tender heart-breaking sex one last time before we got dressed turned to each other one last time before I walked slowly down the winding staircase from her apartment and out into the mysterious orange streetlight and half-darkness. At least a partial parsing of one of her translated poems says as much.

Instead, we had a quiet but gloomy dinner and after I saw her home. She was living rent free on the second floor of a house Wolfgang had found for her through his connections. She opened the gate and walked to the door. She took out her keys and opened the door but did not turn around for one last look. I watched her for a few seconds until the door closed then walked back towards Via Pandolfini where I lived.

What remained was her vague grace, the hushed film-noir way she sometimes looked when she smoked and smiled, poems that hinted at truth and lived on as fiction, her features blurred like an unfocused photograph.

Clara's Books

Here is the only photograph of Clara and I. She is leaning on an old elm tree in front of the house and I am beside a white Anglia. In the photograph she looks sad and vexed, her black curly hair brushed to one side elegant and wild. She is wearing my favorite black T-shirt, the one with a small white eye similar to the one Italian fisherman paint on the bow of their boats to ward off evil when they are out at sea. She stands in a mocking mannequin pose, one of her hands upturned as if she has a stigmata mark. Who took the photo?

The photo was taken at the beginning of September, the time of year when the air is crisp and life seems to start all over again after the sensual languid and dreamy heat of summer.

She is leaning on the tree with her elbow bent, thin and delicate, her big dark eyes merry and sad at the same time. She looks enchanted and distressed, an uncertain woodland nymph, nonchalant but unsure, sensing something in the air, ready to flee.

The photo was taken right after I had taken her for a drive around the block. When I turned right at Arlington Street to head home the passenger door suddenly flew open and almost spilled Clara on to the street.

—This car is a death trap Gabe. Get rid of it. You are going to end up six feet under.

—I just bought it. Is that professor still your friend?

—Oh Gabe, I should never have confided in you. He is a fat pompous fool.

The bloat king of the English department.

—But, you used to like him. You said he was so smart and a writer.

—The key word in that sentence Gabe is 'used to.' I was young then.

Honestly Gabe. Don't worry. He is out of my life. You're not mad are you?

—No, not mad. I was lying.

—Oh, come on Gabe tell it to me straight. What's bothering you? My leaving? Its not like it's a surprise.

—Never mind. Maybe when you come back.

—Ok. You are in such a mood… and she ran her hand through my hair.

—Gabe you have such beautiful hair. She paused.

—Listen, lets not fight. I am going to miss you too but don't worry I will be back for a visit. Find yourself someone while I am gone I won't mind. Plus, lets not forget I am older than…

—Oh, not that again. Please stop it. Anyway, I won't.

—Why not? I am sure there are lots of girls who would love to have you as their boy-friend.

She was incredibly good at deflecting and smoothing things over. The fact she had pretty eyes helped. I did not expect what she said next.

—Find a spot to pull over where no one can see us. Isn't that walled off corner by the funeral home near here?

I liked the way she methodically helped me. Two quick clean tugs and a hand under my butt to help lift it off the car seat and another on my boxers. It was as if I were her baby. She felt both eager and motherly. Two quick tugs and the pants where down around my ankles, then the boxers. She looked down at my center and smiled.

—That was fast. This should help take off your edge.

* * *

My mother had been ill for over a year when Clara arrived at the end of August a year earlier. Clara looked like a fresh innocent school teacher in an old Western movie who had just arrived in a small dusty town, suitcase in hand, and after modestly introducing herself to the ornery sheriff asked where she could find a decent room to stay. But, in reality it was my gruff father doing a bad Italian version of John Wayne. He spoke English with an Italian twang and looked down at his shoes every few seconds unable to make full eye contact with her for long fearing he would betray his hidden appreciation of her looks. Or reveal his mental confusion about why such a pretty single woman wanted to rent a room here. Sugar plum fairies were dancing around his head and it was not even Christmas.

* * *

When Clara moved into the remaining two rooms on the third floor of our three story house there were no bookcases. The ceiling was slanted on both sides, like a Parisian garret she said. The walls were painted hospital white with a single braided light-blub. The kitchen and living room were all rolled into one. On one side was a small sink and a small stove and three kitchen cabinets, the bottom of each stained with cooking smoke. In the other corner was a square stand-up fridge and in the center of the room was a white Formica kitchen table and two mismatched chairs and a worn green couch against the wall. Her other room was a bedroom with a double bed, an old stand-up armoire with a mirror on one of the doors, and a small writing table with a desk lamp placed just where the ceiling began to slant away on an angle. In Clara's imagination there was something of the *Count of Monte Cristo* to the apartment. There was only one small window no bigger than a mandarin orange box in her bedroom which she imagined looked out on the harbor of Marseille. She told me she sometimes dreamed in a whimsical way she was the compassionate and long-suffering Mercedes Mondego, the heroine of the novel.

In fact, you can say everything began and ended with novels and poems with Clara. For me it was the movies, especially old Westerns.

* * *

Both my mother and Clara had been sent into exile although no one in the house knew it except maybe Clara. My mother hour by hour, day by day, in a process similar to geological time, withdrew and eventually separated from my father and I on to her own continent. Clara, on the other hand, had gone into exile to escape a prison. She did not explain.

* * *

Clare at first stored her books in the basement. She had arrived with three full big and tall cardboard boxes to the dismay of my father. We unloaded them and put them along the basement wall that always stayed dry. My father did not understand why she needed so many books but he was impressed. He bragged to his neighbors and brothers a doctor was renting from him. She told my father she was studying to be a doctor but could not provide any advice about my mother's ovarian cancer nor could she get some kind of special care or status for her at the hospital.

How can you be a doctor and own so many books he wondered out loud to me across the dinner-table? I tried to explain but it did not stop him from being suspicious of what she was really up to all day at the university.

* * *

A series of small things gradually broke the distance between us but it would have happened sooner if I was not so dense. The day she sent me down to collect some books from the basement for example. I wasn't able to find her collected works of Lord Byron and so she had to come down to the basement with me to poke around in the pile I had created.

I love the smell of used books. Here smell this, and ran here nose over the open pages.

I did not like the smell – a scent of dust and something moldy – but I kept it to myself. I was keen on her accepting me.

Then there was the time when she forgot her key on one of the coldest days of the winter and stood waiting for my father or I to answer the doorbell which unknown to her was broken for sometime. I finally heard her rapping on the window and rushed to the door like Glen Ford in the Western *Go West, Young Lady.*

Finally, here see how cold it is she said with a merry smile and pressed her frozen lips against mine in the hallway.

I caught the sweet waxy taste of her lipstick and the sour tobacco scent of her breath.

* * *

Clara smoked Cameo menthol cigarettes and when she was out I would get my father's master key and quietly go up the last two short flights of stairs and sneak into her apartment and pinch one from the pack she usually left on the kitchen table. I would sit at the kitchen table and smoke. Looking over the room, I marveled at how she had converted what was a bland room into a little grotto of magic. She had strung blue and white Christmas lights around the ceiling making it festive and look like the night sky when you turned off the main light. The wall posters of a young Bob Dylan and Joan Baez stared at each other from opposite sides of the room. Side by side above the kitchen sink were the Acropolis and a laminated map of Greece. She had covered the light blub so the small room now glowed a honey-brown.

It was also around this time my mother began to see things. I had taken her to to visit the doctor and after the visit we were in the pharmacy when she took off her shoes to avoid all the blood she saw on the floor. It was early November and she was ready to run out the door barefoot on to the snow and half frozen sidewalks. When we got home I went up to Clara's apartment for a smoke.

* * *

I helped Clara put together together the bookcase a week before Christmas. By this point she tired of either sending me down to find some book she needed or having to go down herself. Clara often worked in the middle of the night or when she was unable to sleep she would suddenly remember a letter D.H. Lawrence wrote and how it would fit in nicely with the paper she was writing. Her nocturnal work habits caused a minor uproar on more than one occasion. Clara tried coming down our creaky stairs one foot at a slow time to the basement to find her book but my mother was a light sleeper and slept alone. She shouted out to ask what my father was doing going upstairs in the middle of the night. My father woke and asked her if she was ill or having a nightmare.

Clara slipped into the bathroom to avoid detection.

—Sleep Maria, for the love of God and all the angles. Its only our Doctor or Gabriel using the bathroom. Quiet down. Your shouting is frightening the entire house. Now turn off the light and hush yourself.

—How can I sleep?

Clara then lightly tapped on my door. My room was beside the bathroom on the small second floor landing.

—Gabe are you awake? Do me a favor. I need a book from my stash in the basement Can you go down and get it? I just thought of something. She giggled.

—I'm so sorry I woke everyone up.

The original plan was for my father to assembly the bookcase on the last Saturday before Christmas but he went to the airport to pick up my sister at the last minute and the two of them drove straight to the hospital to see my mother. By this time my mother was in palliative care and my father alternated between morose self-pity and incomprehensibility at the inevitable death of my mother. I instead became numb to everything as a way of avoiding to feel anything. I was afraid if I allowed myself to feel I would be over-whelmed with grief. I was already lost. Clara sensed it.

* * *

After we lay still, out hearts beating fast in spite of the still slow languor that fell over us, a calm like snowflakes falling slowly on the first winter night under a thick low patch of grey. It was a wounded night sky – like us – when she pulled out a book at random from the bookcase and said:

—Open it anywhere and read to me the first thing you see. Read slow, savior the words, catch the control, the spirit of each sentence. How it sounds and feels like fate itself. That there can be no other words except those put in that order at that time. Poems are nets Gabe. Perception and feeling caught.

Over the next weeks and months I read to her many poems and excepts from writers and poets I had never heard of out loud: The opening of Herodotus's *Histories*, Eliot's *Preludes*, Neruda's poem, "Tonight I can Write the Saddest Lines," Anais Nin's *The Delta of Venus*, Auden's poem "Les Beaux Arts," Kroetsch's long poem *The Sad Phoenician*, Ondaatje's *The Cinnamon Peeler*, the middle pages from Militano's novel *Sebastiano's Vine*, the conclusion of Durrell's novel, *Clea*, Homer's the death of Hector in the *Iliad*, Ginsburg's *Howl*. This nowhere near a complete list.

Sometimes she put her ear on my chest to hear how the words effected my heart. Or she put her head just below my chin to hear the music of the words across her ears; sometimes I read to her my finger in her vagina (or rested my palmed hand) so I could feel how the words entered her.

And after, when I stopped reading she would quote Stevens; "She sighed for so much melody."

It was a happy and confusing time.

* * *

I saw the letter inviting her to the University of Toronto on her kitchen table one day when I went up into her apartment for a smoke after returning from the hospice where my mother lay quiet and withdrawn saying nothing. I respected my mother's silence and stared out the window not knowing what to do with her pain, grief, and disappointment. It seemed there was no past or future only the grim present; I was speechless confronted by her blankness and solitude.

I also felt I did not know Clara, the former lovers she embraced. Understanding her was like trying to hold on to a fish in the water and like a fish she kept changing directions.

My mother was lost in a private world, lost in the puzzle of what had become her life: Why cancer? Why was she chosen to suffer? Why the miscarriage long ago?

I did not want to ask the questions because I did not know how to answer them. The out pouring of grief the answers would bring.

As for Clara even though I knew she too had to leave sooner or later, I refused to believe it. It was also difficult to ask her questions.

The room was silent. Blue thin cigarette smoke above the kitchen was part of the interrogation. A small square piece of Marseille sunlight fell on the floor in her bedroom. I wondered how I would be betrayed.

* * *

The photograph at the back of one of my mother's photo albums confuses everything.

How did it get there? My mother was the one who looked after the family pictures starting from baptism to first communion, elementary school, confirmation, birthday parties, weddings, Christmas dinners, picnics at the lake, summer holidays, photos from relatives in Italy. Did I take the photo? How was that possible?

There is also the curious fact Clara left behind the bookcase and a copy each of the *Collected Poems of Wallace Stevens* and the novel *Lady Chatterley's Lover*. She had been writing a paper on the novel for the PMLA, the Modern Language Association of America journal, right up until my mother's death. I remember Clara saying she thought my father's looks reminded her of Mellors, Lady C's lover, whenever she looked down from the balcony at the back of the house where she read seated on a blue towel in a plastic green and white fold-out beach chair in the heat of July and he tended the garden.

By August the basil in the cinder-blocks was a lush green and fragrant, the beans had curled up tall old poles, tomatoes plants were in full bloom spaced and tied in military rows, and a thick carpet of zucchini and cucumbers spread out at the back of the garden. It looked like a scene from a fairy-tale. Rapunzel in the tower?

I had borrowed and read many of Clara's books during my mother's silent struggle and after her death. I had learned reading was an escape away and towards living, how fiction can create life by choosing what to hold up for our examination.

I returned to the rooms where Clara had spent the last sixteen months. There was still a faint scent of her perfume. The posters were there and they continued to stare out at each other. The string of Christmas lights circled the top of the kitchen but in one spot the tape had given way and the lights had slipped down the wall and into a formless loop. She had not washed the bed sheets knowing the stains of our love-making would for a moment return her vividly into my mind.

I picked up and opened the Wallace Stevens collection on the bookshelf. She had bookmarked and underlined the first three lines from the poem "The Idea of Order at Key West."

> She sang beyond the genius of the sea.
> The water never formed to mind or voice
> Like a body wholly body, fluttering

It seemed like a fitting tribute to her leaving and my mother's end. They both had measured solitude and left. I should have told my mother I loved her.

Football Season

Practices were long and hot under a mid-August sun. We crashed and bounced off each other. Peter and I sprinted and carried each other like two-legged camels sweat stinging our eyes. We panted and longed for water. Over and over we ran sweeps, off tackle plays, straight ahead cross blocks. We grunted and groaned at the end of each day. Our bodies ached. Then September's chilly evenings fell like a soft thud. The air turned cool and the light yellow muted and sad at the end of practice. Football season had begun.

I felt self-conscious, and began to worry people at school could detect her scent.

Mrs. Muldoon was a tall Anglo blonde with a pleasing face and large impish blue-grey eyes. She emerged from the water in a black one-piece bathing suit tossing her hair like a lion before a meal. Her teeth flashed an easy white smile full of delight verging on breaking into hilarity. She walked, no she strode, with self-regard and confidence. I could see her firm thighs were covered with goose-bumps, a cold breeze had suddenly come up. She shivered before seating herself in the sun. Her bathing suit was a wet tight black stain. Her bathing suit pulled itself over her firm breasts and visibly outlined her small pea shaped nipples.

She sat cross-legged on a blue and white striped beach blanket and faced the sun in a perfect blank blue sky. Her husband sat at the edge of the blanket on a blonde wooden director's chair with a red cloth back support, his bare-feet planted in the sand. He was reading the paper and smoking a white plastic tipped cigarillo, king of the family archipelago. He sported a beige Panama hat with a black band and blue shorts. His unbuttoned white shirt fluttered in the breeze. Nearby two young teenage girls lay reading shiny gossip magazines under a flamingo pink beach umbrella. Mrs. Muldoon lay with her eyes closed facing the sun, arms stretched back, the valley where her legs met her torso discreetly presented to the world.

I sat on a plain beach towel behind them looking up ever so often from reading Huxley's *Eyeless in Gaza* and watched Mrs. Muldoon. My mother had already retreated from the hot mid-day sun back to our shabby rented cabin on the other side of the narrow asphalt beach road. I had watched her walk away in the simmering heat holding a bit of white cloth over her head. It was barely large enough to keep the sun off the back of her grey-black short curly hair. Father was out for a walk somewhere, his shirt wrapped around his waist, in the direction of town to find a card game in progress at the Venice Café or at least find some unsuspecting tourists to chat their ears off about his troubles. He never tired of complaining about me and mother and our ungrateful attitude towards him.

My parents had rented an inexpensive cottage far from the beach that year.

It faced the highway and was more shack or hut than summer cottage. It was hot day and night and only began to cool off after midnight. The roof had faded grey and black shingles which absorbed the summer heat and the walls were made of cheap pressed wood. During the day my mother opened the front door for a short while before flies and mosquitoes could enter. She also opened the two windows at the back facing a small mini-golf course, and along with the longed for fresh air came the shrieks of people missing their putts.

The cottage came equipped with a big iron wood-burning stove that added to the oppressive heat whenever my unhappy and hard pressed mother took to cooking which was not often. This in turn was another sore point between my parents.

My mother was the opposite of Mrs.Muldoon. Short, dark-haired, mindful of social decorum and religious in a quiet understated way. She never put on a bathing suit. Instead she wore a pair of summer shorts she had made for herself. Her pale thighs were loose and flabby and flamed red instead of tanning if exposed too long in the sun. She never bared her shoulders and made sure her back was always covered even on relentless summer afternoons.

She also despaired about my father's gambling, his relentless need to find release from home and work, his countless unexplained late nights.

An atmosphere of freedom and tolerance, casual wealth, and ease surrounded the Muldoon family. They were indifferent to everything and everyone around them. The looked like a secure cocooned family. A copy of her 'Architect Magazine' lay at the feet of Mrs. Muldoon, its pages turning in the breeze. It added to the image of an artistic and moneyed family.

The Muldoon's owned a big cottage with a chimney made from large pink and grey stones cut perfect from what appeared to be the Neolithic age. The wrap around veranda faced the old marina. Below the veranda the lawn rolled away from the house in a series of small green waves. On both sides of the stone path leading up to the house from the drive-way were a series of neat and evenly spaced garden flowers.

Peter Muldoon had showed up to football practice on the

third day. He drove his father's vintage 1964 green MG. The car was a marvel: wooden floor-boards, polished wood steering wheel, chrome-spokes, beautiful curves and wide fenders. On the dashboard, uncluttered black and white dials.

He had offered to give me a ride home. I asked him to drop me off downtown far from my old and depilated Langside Street home then caught the bus home.

Peter had his mother's large eyes and his father's wide brow and firm chin. Fawn eyes in a man's head was something most young teenage girls find irresistible. Peter also carried himself like an ancient Greek god and smiled like an actor. The entire combination gave him the ability to lift private-school teen age girl's dresses up past their waist or he was able to slip a hand down after a short and careless pursuit on weekends. I was envious of his conquests but was never really in awe as he hoped.

On a pale grey and white Saturday afternoon in early November before our last regular season game – the one that would decide whether or not we would get into the play-offs – we drove to the Park Restaurant after practice. It was his treat, since as per usual, I was broke.

—Peter, what the hell. Very funny ha-ha-ha. Are you crazy...

I had to push him away before getting out of the car and laughed thinking it was some kind of dumb joke. It was totally unexpected.

He frowned and said nothing but instead of stopping for a bite he abruptly drove off in furious silence down Route 90 and over the St. James Bridge. He pulled up to the Viscount-Gort Hotel where I often met his mother on the weekends.

—Get out, he shouted and then sped away, the car lurching forward as if possessed.

He changed gears sharply and blew through the Stop sign

at the end of the parkade. I was embarrassed. He knew and I wondered when and how he found out. I thought of phoning his mother and telling her what happened.

Later, he had parked the MG on a side of the road on Wilkes Avenue and waited. He then got out of the car and walked towards the train on the main-line.

The accident was reported in the news the next morning. We went ahead and played that afternoon and lost. Everything over forever.

Alex's Funeral

I took out the plastic baggie with a zip-lock from the gold and silk coloured Chinese handbag embroidered with a red dragon and orange fish Anne's husband had given to me to carry Alex in. I poured him out, a fine white and blue-gray powder, underneath the low branches of a wild Maple tree that had grown half-way down the hill known as Westview Park. I put the small old St. Christopher medal Ann gave me on a branch above him.

Westview Park used to be know as Garbage Hill when we were kids, on Sundays in the winter it was a great place to go tobogganing. I figured he would appreciate the view. The tree looked out towards the West End where he had lived his entire life. Directly in front of us were the fine middle-class bungalows of the West End. Far in the distance were the low rent inner city streets of Young, Spence, Furby, and Langside, and the ragged jumble of Ellice and Sargent. Each Avenue was fitted with small red-bricked corner grocery stores, faded bakeries, hairdressing salons, shabby hardware stores, and pawn shops. When Alex and I were growing up there was even an old movie theatre on Ellice near Sherbrook – The Max – and on a Saturday afternoon you could see two feature films for twenty cents and spend your remaining nickel on a horrible piece of candy called Roman Nougat. None of this mattered anymore.

I poured out the ashes and Paul said a few words about

how Alex showed him how to think outside of the box. I read a stanza from a Pessoa poem – Alex liked to read but I don't think he was much of a poetry fan unless it was the lyrics of a rock band, he was stoned, and feeling bluesy. I then read the opening six lines from 'You Can't Always get What You Want', one of Alex's favorite Rolling Stones songs. I remembered when we were young watching Alex mouth 'I saw her today at the reception, a glass of wine in her hand...', his fingers had formed a soft fist and clutched a cigarette. He held a beer in his other hand as if it was a grenade. We had paused for a cigarette break after a serious round of smoking hash from a homemade water pipe in Tom's room upstairs.

Paul and I walked back up the hill. We stopped to take in the view. Two women were coming up the road walking their dogs. They glanced over at us and looked puzzled at what two men where doing walking up the side of the hill so early in the morning without dogs and then pausing to gaze out towards downtown. A thin, grey, low fog had rolled in. Unusual for August in Winnipeg. It hung over the downtown like a widow's veil from turn of the century Warsaw. Fitting I thought. Alex's parents were Polish. The green tops of elm and ash trees spread out in a relentless march towards downtown. The thin haze muted the box shapes of the sky-scrappers at the corner of Portage and Main. You could also see the square outlines of the apartments near Central Park. The buildings silhouetted in the grey mist looked fake and hollow like large forgotten facades. The weather seemed made for the occasion.

—You are a good friend to do this for him.

—I didn't want to do it. Thanks for agreeing to help. I am not sure I have done the right thing or if I am a great friend. Its bizarre how Ann just handed me over half of him. I drove around with half of him in my trunk for two weeks. Ann says she is going to gather up a group and pour the other half of his remains under a tree he used to like in a park near Assiniboine Park. She is also planning a party, some kind of celebration of Alex's life.

We got in the car and drove off the hill. We talked about how strange and tragic Alex's end turned out to be. Both his parents and older brother dead before him. As a result, there was no one to look after him or see him in the hospital except for a handful of old friends, some near, some far away. Ann, Alex's ex-partner, and her husband looked after him throughout his illness. There was also Gwen. She used to live in an old apartment on Maryland Street near Westminster Church. Alex and I visited her years ago one winter afternoon for reasons that remain obscure. Probably for a drink and a toke. Ann had brought Gwen up in conversation before.

—Gwen was there when he died. I had left about hour earlier.

—Gwen?

—Yes, Gwen Thomas. They kept in touch.

—Dirty Blonde-haired Gwen? I think she became a single mom at a young age.

—Yes, that's her. Her kid is all grown up now. You know Alex remained friends with almost all of his ex-girl-friends.

—Oh, was the best I could reply.

My own friendship with Alex began back in elementary when I was an awkward new kid in class in a new school. One day out of the blue he asked me over to his place for a Saturday afternoon. I was eager to make new friends and accepted Alex's offer.

His home had a rec-room in the basement lined with faux dark wood. Alex and his older brother Richard shared the room. In one corner was Richard's small writing desk littered with scarps of paper and an ashtray usually half full with cigarette butts. In the centre of the room was an old red Persian carpet. Jutting out from each wall were two built in couches to lie on, read or sit. Underneath one of the couches was a secret compartment were Richard hid his Playboy stash. Nearby, under a tall bronze lampstand with a gold coloured lampshade and green strip, sat a portable record player on a small table with a neat stack of records on the side mostly bought by Richard. On the main bookshelf and all the window sills were horror-movie models, military airplanes, battleships, and quirky monsters. Alex had painstakingly painted and glued together all of them. Black and pale Frankenstein with bolts in his neck, the moss green Creature from the Black Lagoon, British, American, and Nazi planes, ships each with their specific military insignias flawlessly painted. But his pride and joy was a hideous and mysterious looking green chunk of paper Mache flecked with yellow paint spots. At the top the curved head of coat hanger jutting out. The green misshapen blog hung from on a short string near the entrance to the laundry room.

—Guess what it is. He pointed to the hanging slab of green.

—No clue.

—I'll give you a hint. I made it out of flour and strips of newspapers. Home-made Mache.

I looked again. It looked like a large piece of deformed newsprint painted green. You could make out the faded bits of light grey newsprint under the paint. I shrugged.

—It's snot. Get it? he said and then smirked.

We returned to the rec room and he reached under one of the couches, slide back a panel and pulled out a Playboy magazine.

His mother called us up to the kitchen for lunch. He grabbed the magazine from my hand and quickly returned it to the secret drawer.

Here was another surprise. His mother had made ham and cheese sandwiches with potato chips, a pickle, and a glass of coke.

I drew the obvious conclusion that Alex and his mother were modern Europeans who lived a charmed life. They appeared to have stepped right out of a T.V. Guide compared to my still freshly minted immigrant family. We had no reference points in the New World nor cared to gather them up. Instead we remained, least my parents remained, rooted in their memories of what they had left behind.

Why this sudden memory of first meeting him? It was pointless. The awful fact was he was dead before I could say good-bye. He died with a rare horrible disease, mind gone, his body in the end a skeleton tattooed with purple blotches all over his arms and legs. All the music, books, booze and drugs pointless.

It was his ending as much as our erratic friendship that I could not stop thinking about. Nor could I prevent myself from thinking that from an early age he had showed himself to be a quirky artist but had crushed that impulse. Alex sought and then crushed the spiritual and artist awareness he found in drugs and booze, records, and books. He cultivated an odd hard-boiled cynicism about himself and other people. But his cynicism, like all cynics, masked a real desire to connect and be connected to other people. The material world and its attractions be damned. There was also a yearning, or a dissatisfaction. He masked it by mocking people and having an eye for the odd and twisted. The unusual in life. I only now recognize it for what it was: a shield.

* * *

I dropped Paul off and drove through the old West End neighbourhood. I was having a difficult time recalling my past with Alex. Perhaps youth is a fairy-tale or its recalled as if a dream. The best you can hope for is to remember some incident, some day that unfolded like a play with a beginning, middle, and end that was either funny or tragic. Or absurd. Or incomprehensible. The only thing you can say for sure is you were there.

I drove past the corner not far from Alex's parents home where I drank half a bottle of rum when I was fourteen and in the rush of the cold night air promptly threw up in front of a pair of stopped cars. Now there is a Portuguese club and café where we used to play pool and order fries. Just past Victor Street is where an old man sat at the end of two rows of bookshelves lined with used books. He wore wireless glasses on his gaunt pale face and always was dressed in a white and blue stripped shirt with silver shirt bands that puffed his sleeves like a medieval courtier. He wore a blue tie, and grey wool pants regardless of the weather. We thought he looked like an ex-Nazi colonel in hiding. He never smiled, never spoke, was suspicious of twelve-year-old customers, Alex and I, always asking for used Sargent Rock comic books. Later as teenagers we bought paperbacks, usually spy thrillers by Len Deighton or Lawrence Block, *The Cancelled Czech*, a favorite. In spite of our shared past we drifted away from each other.

This too is hard to pinpoint. How and why our friendship lost its footing. It troubled me that I was unable to say why or when. Our lives became busy? Busy explains nothing. Our habits changed after my marriage? Gwen? Gwen and I had still kept in touch but Alex never came up. It had been so long ago. He had several affairs after her but never talked about them. He had lived with Ann. Whenever I saw him again he seemed to be repressing his torment. Regrets? Whatever it was there was a coiled spring of emotion that he pushed down. He said little about his health or how he spent his days over the few lunches I had with him. The medication made him moody. His remained stubborn and discreet about the past or present for that matter. Flashes of bitter sarcasm flared. It was his way of maintaining his dignity but also meant the present was hollow.

I saw him infrequently. Now and again a word or two drifted back to me about how he had changed jobs, or about the unexpected passing of his older brother. His heavy drinking, then moderate drinking, then finally his disease and pride at not letting anyone know he was dying. I visited him in the hospital after Ann contacted me. One of my last images is Alex in bed holding his dick and shouting pee, pee. Shortly before this I had found him locked into a chair in the hall shouting at the nurses, fuck off, fuck off.

He died while I was away in the Algarve.

Gwen ignored my messages about his death. Her silence both surprised and disappointed me. It was so strange how his adult years became a mystery, how time did little to reveal him. How his life was a prologue to nothing.

It must have been unbearable. I still look for clues.

The Artist

The English Department Chair – a tall man with a neatly trimmed V-shaped Edwardian beard and stern demeanor – agreed to allow me to be an Honors student on a conditional basis for one year. His slow serious nods and firm voice projected a seriousness about the matter at hand. I simply wanted a change. I was bored and failing at the memory work required to be a successful Psychology student. I also possessed a slow burning curiosity about art with a capital A. Working class kid reaching for sophistication and worldliness was also in the mix.

There was also the strange mystical, and exotic land of poetry. Maybe I could become a poet as a side benefit. I had already tasted the complicated fruit of Leonard Cohen, T.S. Eliot, and Dylan Thomas.

My turn towards literature was therefore an obvious decision over a beer with Alex one late night in June at the old Camelot Bar on Portage Avenue.

—You like to read, so why not?

—Sure, but what the hell do you do with an English degree?

—Probably end up working in a shoe store.

Literature would set me apart from the common herd, confer on me the special status of being a creative individual, and on a less elevated level I believed it would include the added bonus of making me attractive to females. Of course, I did not know much about suffering artists and that rarely were they considered attractive to most women. Even suffering female artists did not care much for them. Still, I believed life would be more real, more fun as an artist in progress. The study of art and culture, reading and writing, and talking about books seemed like a way to towards my real or at least an ideal self but what I wanted most was my real self, whatever that was. I also desperately wanted a purpose, and a ticket out and away from the tedium of want I saw as a middle-class future.

The script, unknown to me, was predictable much in the same way French intellectuals are preoccupied with rattling the bourgeoisie cages of society they came from and eventually settled into bourgeois life. The problem was I was a working class kid.

Two months before changing programs I met Judy.

Judy's eyes were set in a circle of two dark purple rings and she pulled on her fizzy brown hair in an unconscious and distracted way as we talked. She was not good-looking in the conventional sense but I was impressed by the way she puckered her lips as she exhaled cigarette smoke. She drank her beer in quick full bursts tilting her head on an angle. She watched me carefully talking to her without betraying what she really thought of me, or what I was going on about. I was surprised when she accepted my proposal to go away on the Labour Day weekend knowing next to nothing about me. I surprised myself by asking. I immediately went out and bought a two-man mountain tent that when set up looked like a long rolled out blue condom.

We spent our camping weekend cooking so-so food over the campfire and only on the last day did we go into town for some decent Chinese food. We played the I Chin book to see what the future held for us and what it said about our personalities. This added to the growing fiction we were both mystic and mysterious and noble since we were together without sex. We tried but she mumbled something about a fallen vagina making sex painful.

Both of us could not imagine sex without intercourse. Oral sex was a ground breaking event, even a taboo. So we spent our time in the tent reading and not talking much. The sunlight bounced off the lake and a quiet unassuming melancholy fell over her. I adopted a cool attitude that I was interested in her above and beyond sex. We somehow signaled to each to other that not talking much was a sign we were meant for each other. We were a soft-spoken couple. Perhaps, we were both living up to be the opposite of the loud everyday strife in our families.

So after the weekend, the relationship continued to bumble along with my feelings more and more disconnected from her and finding my longings reflected in the poetry of John Donne. We went for cheap dinners in the Osborne Village, there was a place that sold meatball sandwiches out of the back of a garage, and went for walks along the paths in Assiniboine Park to take in the fall colors. The chill in the air said winter was coming. It was all nice but felt empty and pointless.

In November Judy decided to have a party. Remembrance day had fallen on a Friday so Judy decided to have a party Thursday night.

I arrived late and was let into the apartment by Gloria her plump roommate.

—Sorry, I' m late. The place sounds packed.

—Come in Marco. Judy just went out to buy cigarettes and some more dip

—She was expecting you to help set up. No matter. I am

sure she will be glad you made it. Drinks are in the kitchen.

The fact of the matter was I was thinking of breaking up with Judy but changed my mind. I was angry with myself for being so indecisive. The minute I walked through the door I was reminded how the relationship felt stale and arid. I stood in the hallway and handed my winter jacket to Gloria and felt awkward playing the role of Judy's sincere boy-friend. Gloria scooped my six-pack of beer and headed down the hall to the kitchen and I stepped around the corner towards the music and loud buzz of chatter coming from the living room. I cast an eye around the room hoping to recognized some one.

She was wearing a black leather skirt, all the other women wore jeans. She had a soft purple mohair sweater that followed and flowed faultlessly over the curved slopes of her evenly shaped breasts. I could not see her face. The side of her head was tilted towards someone sitting on the floor, drink in one hand, white pale cigarette in the other listening. Her hair fell like a thin blonde curtain around the side of her head making it impossible to see her face. She eventually pulled her head back and after a quick impatient animal shake of the head her hair fell back over her shoulders revealing cool sad blue-grey eyes, a pair of small round delicate cheekbones and a wide brow. Her mouth was expressionless. There was a patrician look to her, intellectual and self-possessed. Who was she?

I watched her for most of the evening and noted she did not play backgammon nor take much of an interest in the I Ching everyone had tried at least once. She did take a long studied look at a summer photo album that was being passed around. It was then I realized that she had worked with Judy at the same summer job up North.

Around midnight people began to leave in twos and threes. Outside an unexpected snow fall had started. It was snowing hard and you can hear the wind pass through the tall summer screens left on the windows. Judy was drunk. She pushed me into the bathroom to talk.

—Stay. We can cuddle. I'll make you a fab brekie in the morning.

—Bacon and iggs, she slurred.

I inwardly groaned. Judy then opened the door and stumbled down the hall towards her bedroom. I did not follow.

The purple mohair girl was leaving. I decided to ask her if she needed a ride home. The weather had changed for the worse. Snow was now falling fast and thick. The wind in short, heavy gusts pushed the snow around.

—Need a ride?

—Well, I was thinking of calling a cab. Oh, ok. Why not?

I put on my coat and watched her search for her winter boots lost in a pile of shoes from the remaining party guests; tucked in the corner, neat and aloof, I recognized Judy's lonely brown winter boots.

Her elbow caught the end of her leather skirt as she tugged on her black boot. It lifted her skirt for a moment past her thigh and I turned away to light a cigarette pretending not to notice. She caught my gesture and smiled.

We drove down River Avenue to Osborne Street, and then right towards the Osborne Bridge. We silently smoked as the car crossed the bridge.

The Assiniboine River was not completely frozen. You could see large dark open black patches of water. The trees along the bank were thick and inked against a blank sky. Snow fell in irregular slants on the the Legislature making its Roman Corinthian columns vague and ethereal; the green bronze classical dome and its forgotten nod to the mausoleum of Halicarnassus surreal under the falling snow and wind.

At the corner by the The Bay we turned on to Portage Avenue. The avenue was desolate and windswept. At a red light the white exhaust poured from a car in front of us. The exhaust danced, appeared and disappeared in the the wind like a mad genie. An empty bus all lit up with white light purred loudly.

We drove down Main Street towards the North End. She lived on Atlantic between Main and Salter. Main looked exhausted. Streetlamps gave off a dull washed out orange light. A few drunks staggered down the street like the undead, in spite of the weather, from one run-down hotel towards the next.

Inside the car we slowly began talking about ourselves. We handed over our ethnic origins and status like passports.

She was Polish. Her parents had met near the end of the Second World War in Italy where her mother was a nurse and her father a member of the Polish Free Army fighting with the British at Monte Casino. Her father had been wounded at Monte Casino. Her parents met in a field hospital and married after the war. There was not much to go back to in Poland. Plus, the communists had taken over. Britain offered free passage to veterans to the former colonies of Canada or Australia. Her parents choose Canada and Winnipeg in particular because her mother had an aunt who had settled in the city before the war. Much later when she was born they named her Victoria in memory of their contribution to the victory in Europe. As a Fine Arts student she admired the work of Wanda Koop, a local artist born in the North End like her. She loved Miro, the Russian painter Kandinsky, and Egyptian tomb art.

—What are you interested in?

—I'm a newly minted English student.

—What are you going to do with an English degree?

—Good question.

She expressed her art preferences like the curator of a small art gallery sizing up an artist. Her tone was measured with a hint of distant haughtiness. Her high-minded tone expressed a seriousness about art I had never encountered before. It impressed me and mirrored my simmering desire to know more about art. It was also the opposite of my nagging self-doubt and uncertainty about my future. It also suggested sophisticated appreciation, something I only knew second hand from books and film, mainly French.

This was a long pause.

Coffee?

Sure. There is a little place on Inkster just off Main that should be open.

* * *

I was squeezing a small half opened plastic cream container into my coffee when it and her reserve finally broke. The cream landed on my black sweater.

She snorted and let out a quick loud laugh, stopped herself, and then suppressed a giggle.

—You sure aren't trying to impress me with how cool you are. Different from most guys I meet.

I continued to wipe away ignoring her laughter.

—I am not going to say what that looks like. She giggled again.

I was pleased my accident made her laugh. Her laughter felt real and suggested another version of herself, warmer and easier to know, less encased in the fake armor of art school detachment. It felt for a moment like some kind of victory to make a quiet reserved pretty woman you met for the first time laugh. I also noted her sly sexual innuendo and the experience it suggested.

The next day Judy called me to talk about the party. It could have been a moment of truth but I repeatedly failed the truth test with her. I wanted to ask her about Victoria but this too would have been trouble.

We both pretended nothing of consequence had happened. She apologized for going to bed drunk and did not seem to remember asking me to stay over.

I soon began giving Victoria a ride home from university after her classes in print-making and drawing. I studied and waited for her in the Architecture Library. She disliked both of her evening classes. She especially disliked her Drawing Professor. He had made several passes at her and offered pompous critiques of her work.

—He is such a fool. He thinks my drawings are all wrong. Not all women are wildly hairy down there or have the right curves.

She then pressed her lips into a mischievous grin.

—Take me. I sometimes shave and end up looking like a little girl.

Her comment left me daft for the rest of the drive home. I smoked two cigarettes in a row. She hardly seemed to recognize the effect of her playfulness nor did she seem to care. I eventually pulled over and masturbated in the car after I dropped her off. I let the tissue fly out the window as I drove home. I watched it flutter free into a snow bank, the sperm soaked table napkin now a naughty part of yet another layer of Winnipeg winter.

* * *

My hunger for art and its promise of freedom began a year earlier after my visit to Paris and the Louvre. The grandeur, romanticism, and sheer power of the wall size paintings by Delacroix, David, and Ingres on two exhaustive afternoons in the middle of August in Paris opened me up to the idea of Art as a noble pursuit. Art was beyond the mundane concerns of the material world and it celebrated its immortality over and over again. And then there was Paris itself.

I walked purposeless through the Tuileries Garden lined full of stately statues and vases and neatly trimmed elms and mulberry trees and eventually arrived at the open expanse of Place de la Concorde, and its sparkling fountains, frenetic traffic disorder, grand aristocratic buildings, and in the center of it all an Egyptian obelisk stolen by Napoleon painted black, the ancient hieroglyphs gold.

Wide-eyed, cautious, and self-conscious I walked down Boulevard Saint-Germain past outdoor cafes full of well-dressed Parisian and émigrés intellectuals, or so I imagined. Followed the twists and turns of Rue de Buci to Place St. Michel and gazed at the green bronze archangel and its small fountain lions. After an espresso, I walked down Rue Saint-Severin to finally rest at a small café on Rue de la Harpe late at night under the gaze of a pretty woman and her lover. I was thrilled to overhear her whisper into her lover's ear 'c'est un ecrivain' after she saw me scribbling into a notebook.

The next day I crossed the Pont Neuf and walked to Notre Dame, then back towards the Champs-Elysees but not before wandering along the Quai Voltaire and the bookstalls on the Left Bank. I returned exhausted to my shabby hotel on Rue de l'Ancienne Comedie and tried to read Miller's 'Tropic of Cancer' half grasping his vain quest to be a writer, and pondered the mysterious use of the bidet. On the half worn out carpeted floor lay a map of Paris all marked up with the streets I had walked. I took a nap, woke and splashed cold water on my face, peed at the end of the hall, and I was out the door and down the stairs to eat a cheap hardy Serbian stew at Restaurant des Balkans as the evening light fell. I watched the Parisian streets turn grey and white and full of shapeless shadow; the street lights made the round heads of cobble-stones shine. I walked checked once again my thick wad of French francs – my entire cash for ten days – against my thigh. It made me feel temporarily secure every time I checked, most of my money hidden in a secret pocket sown by my mother on my underwear. The city, like my hidden money, was one big secret I wanted to uncover.

* * *

It crossed my mind more than once I should let Judy know I was no longer interested in her. I wanted a lover – like my conception of art – free and grand to explore and conquer the future. Someone smart, funny, and free-spirited but I was un-able to say this without feeling ridiculous.

Victoria was not funny, although she did like a saucy joke, which I mistook for a free-spirit. My view of her intelligence was based on the fact she could do something grand: paint and draw. By now I had absorbed enough half-baked ideas about Art to be drawn into her self-conception and self-drama as a suffering misunderstood soul yearning to be an artist. Her longing matched mine and her sadness was part and parcel of the noble siren call of Art. I did not know real artistic achievement included a long apprenticeship, repeated failure, persistence, and ego. It also helped to have a bit of luck.

As I learned more about her and her family the more her sadness seemed high-minded, noble. I hid my desire from her. I understood her suffering and desire to be an artist as complex and it included silence, pride, and rejection. It is a mystery to me why this added to her allure. She was pretty. How could anyone reject her? She told me she had an abor-tion at fifteen, and her mother drew the obvious conclusion that she was a slut. Her mother never forgave her. Her father escaped the drama and shame by working late as a cabdriver. At the end of the night he played cards in late night booze cans. Her art professors were lechers through and through, and her older sister wrote her off as a snob and unrealistic romantic playing at being an artist.

Without realizing it, I had been cast in the role of white knight.

Her repressed sexuality, intense desire to be an artist and to move beyond her drab working-class beginnings added to her appeal, her purity. Here she was a sad and scorned pretty woman cast adrift in the world. It made her seem soulful. Her tragic soulfulness combined with her pretty face and body made her alluring. But, why? A desire to save myself in an effort to save her? I wondered how much she was conscious of her effect on me. Her need to be saved and my desire for her were at odds.

The snow fell again and again that winter sometimes soft and still hushing the city except for the whoosh of tires on the wet streets. Or the snow came fast, furious from the North-West, slithering along the frozen streets like long thin white snakes. And it didn't matter at all if she did not love me. I had fallen in love with her sadness, her wounded soul. I was a vessel into which she had poured her grief. It changed how I saw the world. She saw everything through a melancholy gauze. I misunderstood this melancholy as the reality and purpose of art. I wanted to see beyond the everyday surfaces, the monotony and tedium of the practical and expose what I believed was the loneliness at the core of every life and live authentically. This is where art began I thought.

A few weeks later on a blank New Year's Eve she guided our hands together under her jeans and past her cotton briefs to arrive at the top her pubic bone. The entire moment was so natural I was barely able to register it. My hand sat still on her middle as if on a patch of wet grass. She began to rock back and forth then her middle parted ever so slightly so that one of my fingers on its own accord slipped into her. She shut her eyes and moaned under her breath. She was in a delicious trance. This lasted for what felt like an eternity but was probably no more than a few minutes. I heard the door squeak near the kitchen. I turned and saw someone looking out at us from the dark narrow gap between the closed kitchen door and the wall. Victoria at that very moment shuddered and fell onto my neck and shoulder and gasped. Her small chest moved in fast irregular beats on top of me; She was breathing hard into my ear. A few hot tears fell on my neck. Her long blonde hair had formed a partial veil across my eyes. I looked again. Her mother's eyes were gone. We both lay still, my arm across her back. No one spoke. The house so silent you could hear the cold. I said nothing about what I saw.

Dazed she got up from the top of me and went straight up the stairs to her room without a word.

I found my coat in the hall and stumbled into the crisp cold early morning of a new year. Small white stars were neatly tacked up in all their rightful places. Orion stood posed, arm at the ready, at his post on the immense blue sky. The night was still, empty and filled with what seemed like an immutable order. The cold felt inhuman and gave everything a bitter cold clarity. I drove home through the frozen empty streets thinking what had I seen? Done? It felt like a Hitchcock moment, strangely perverse. A long invisible shadow from the past was there, and a ghost in the form of a wound that only the sad quest for beauty and art could transform, cure, and after many years turn into a short story or painting.

The problem is art is always incomplete. I would learn this later.

Her orgasm and her pilgrim quest for art were about finding freedom, experiencing desire, creating a new ego. We both were unknowingly trying to escape and find direction, and for me at least, past what I though was bland awareness and my chaotic immigrant past. I was also seeking relief from many empty and cold journeys into the night, to replace the void I had created by rejecting pretty much everything except for art but unable to replace. Instead, I was curious and wanted to solve the mystery at the core of literature which I had mistaken for the key to unlocking life.

It was a short drive over the Redwood Bridge. I glanced at the frozen white and wind swept river below. It had no philosophy, no theory to explain. The cold remained silent, the empty city streets in its grip. No answers.

I had fallen in love with melancholy and silence.

Acknowledgments:

An excerpt from the short story "An Oneiric Education" called "To Shed Our Impossible Grief" was originally published in *The Dream Machine*, an on-line journal, International Edition, November, 2017, Bologna, Italy, edited by Pina Piccolo.

My thanks to Michael Carrino for his careful reading of the stories and suggestions and Steve Synder for encouragement.

As always for my parents Carmela Foti and Domenico Militano, and Vera, Adrianna, Tony, Rosa, and Pina.

Carmelo Militano is an award winning poet & writer. He won the F.G. Bressani award for poetry in 2004 for his chapbook *Ariadne's Thread*. (Olive Press, 2003). His poetry includes the collections *Morning After You* (Ekstasis Editions,2014) and *The Stone Mason's Notebook* (Ekstasis Editions, 2016). Militano's novel *Sebastiano's Vine* (Ekstasis Editions, 2103), was short-listed for the Margaret Laurence fiction prize and his non-fiction work *The Fate of Olives* (Olive Press, 2006) was also short-listed. His reviews, essays, and literary interviews have appeared in journals across Canada. Militano currently hosts and produces the P.I. New Poetry show, CKUW 95.9 FM, University of Winnipeg. *Lost Aria* is his fifth book.